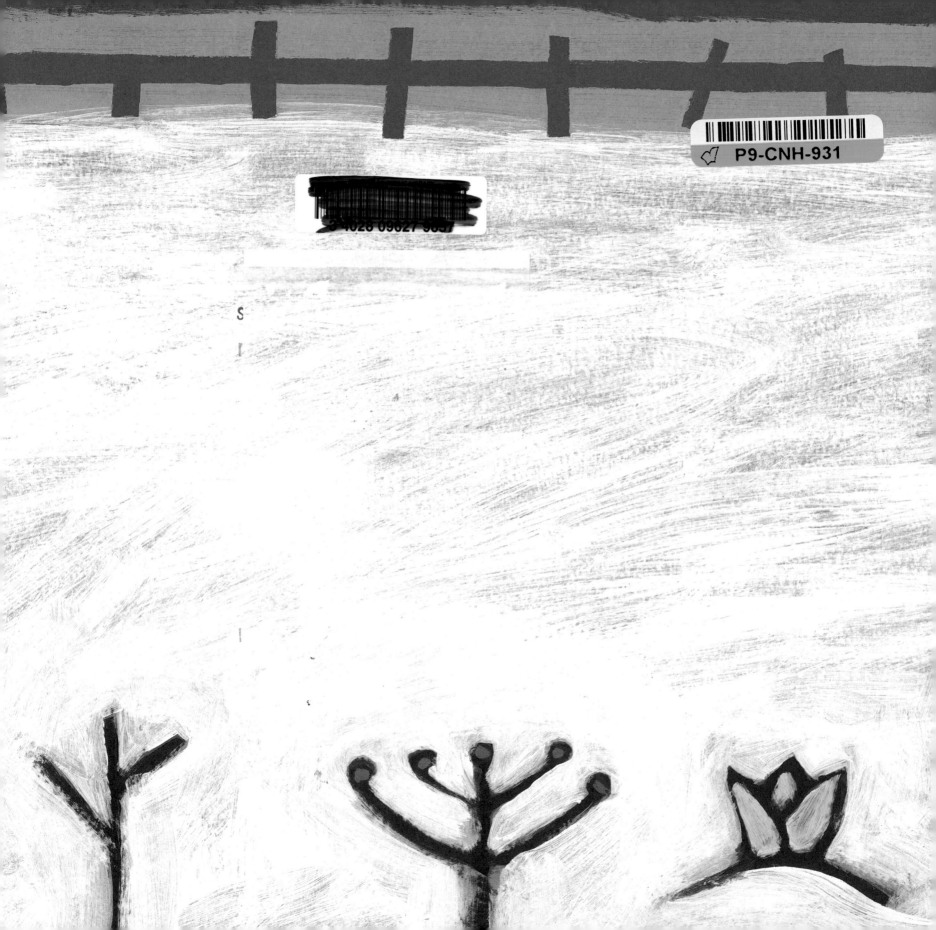

CLEO IN THE SNOW

Caroline Mockford

Barefoot Books
Celebrating Art and Story

Cleo wakes, Cleo winks.

Cleo yawns, Cleo blinks.

Cleo goes outside.
Cleo stops to stare.

The garden is all
white and cold,
with snowflakes
everywhere.

Cleo sniffs,
Cleo swipes,

Caspar sniffs,
Caspar bites.

"Caspar, let's go
for a ride.

Come and sit with me!"

Caspar
swiftly
sleds
downhill.

Cleo watches warily.

"Come on Cleo,
it's your turn."

Cleo has a ride.

For Poppy — S. B.
For Talia and Matya — C. M.

Barefoot Books
3 Bow Street, 3rd Floor
Cambridge, MA 02138

First published in the United States of America in 2002 by Barefoot Books, Inc.

This book has been printed on 100% acid-free paper
The illustrations were prepared in acrylics on 140lb watercolor paper
Design by Jennie Hoare, England
Typeset in 44pt Providence Sans Bold
Color separation by Bright Arts Graphics, Singapore
Printed and bound in Singapore by Tien Wah Press Pte Ltd

1 3 5 7 9 8 6 4 2

Library of Congress Cataloging-in-Publication Data   (U.S.)
       Blackstone, Stella.
            Cleo in the snow / [Stella Blackstone] ; Caroline Mockford.-
       1st ed.
       [24] p. : col. ill. ;   cm.   (Cleo the cat)
       Note: The moral right of Stella Blackstone to be identified as the author
       and Caroline Mockford to be identified as the illustrator of this work
       has been asserted. [last page of text]
       Summary: Cleo the kitten and Caspar the puppy play in the snow for
       the very first time and enjoy an exciting sledding ride that proves to be
       a little too exciting for them.
       ISBN 1 84148-951-4
       1. Cats - Fiction. 2. Dogs - Fiction. 3. Stories in rhyme.
       4. Friendship - 1. Mockford, Caroline. 11. Title. 111. Series.
    [E] 21 2002   AC   CIP

Barefoot Books
Celebrating Art and Story

At Barefoot Books, we celebrate art and story with books that open the hearts and minds of children from all walks of life, inspiring them to read deeper, search further, and explore their own creative gifts. Taking our inspiration from many different cultures, we focus on themes that encourage independence of spirit, enthusiasm for learning, and acceptance of other traditions. Thoughtfully prepared by writers, artists, and storytellers from all over the world, our products combine the best of the present with the best of the past to educate our children as the caretakers of tomorrow.

www.barefootbooks.com